A Burning Secret

Beverly Montgomery

ISBN: 978-0-578-11730-0

DEDICATION

This book is dedicated to all of you who continue to read and be interested in my books. Without you, there would be no need for me to write.

ACKNOWLEDGMENTS

My inspiration is my family who always encourages and inspires me. I wouldn't be where I am today without your support!

CHAPTER ONE

It is the year 1970 and Montclair City is full of excitement! Located outside of New York City, it is a beautiful and progressive city and people from all parts of the world come here to have a great time!

Downtown Montclair is saturated with a variety of cafes' and restaurants, jazz and blues clubs, and shopping boutiques.

There is something for everyone to do and especially tourists but the city has its share of crime so one does have to be careful.

All across the country, there is a section of society living in communes and they are referred to as hipsters. They are great advocates of free love and their motto is, *"Make Love and Peace."*

They have an overwhelming opposition to the status quo and are committed to challenging it.

It is simply a different time and in many ways a very exciting time to be alive!

When shopping in Downtown Montclair, it is not unusual to see women dressed elegantly while lingering on the streets, window shopping and patronizing sidewalk cafés. The aroma of hot croissants and coffee consume the air.

Many tourists frequent playhouses to enjoy the latest and greatest stage plays and are awed and captivated with performances by their favorite actors and actresses of the day.

But in lower Montclair, on Bermuda Street, lives Callie Broadway, a single mother and her daughter Sasha.

Callie is a very beautiful woman and it is clear that her daughter Sasha has gotten her great looks from her.

Callie was once heavily involved and caught up in the *Love and Peace Movement*.

At the time, she was dating Sasha's father Gregory Callahan whom she met when she attended Bismarck College in New York.

Gregory and Callie were very much in love with being in love and caught up in the times and all that it enveloped.

They were majoring in Political Science when they met Melanie Spencer, a young woman with strong political and social beliefs. Melanie even participated in several war protests.

It was Melanie who persuaded Gregory and Callie to go with her to visit Belleview Village, a large commune on the outskirts of New York City.

There they saw large groups of people with different lifestyles and cultures vocalizing their disdain for the war and other political and social issues.

Gregory and Callie were intrigued by the people residing in the commune and decided to take a year off from college to join them.

But their decision was fraught with a number of problems that they hadn't counted on.

The most pressing issue was their lack of money for food and other necessities.

At college, they didn't have to worry about room and board and they had access to food because the students in their dorms often shared food and whatever else could be shared among them.

Gregory found a way to support himself and Callie by making a variety of wooden artifacts which he sold on the streets in Belleview Village.

And they both participated in the cultivation of a variety of fruits and vegetables that they sold at the local Farmer's Market.

But there was an unexpected problem arising between the men in the commune because Gregory had a bad roving eye and the women in the commune were enchanted with his good looks.

His mistake was getting it on with one of the leaders' old lady and he threatened to throw

Gregory out on his butt if he dared to even look at his old lady again.

Callie didn't care what Gregory did because she was too busy doing her own thing.

Then to make matters worse, Callie got pregnant and Gregory wanted little to do with her.

But when the baby was born, Gregory felt sorry for her and agreed to sign as the father, on the baby's birth certificate.

Callie was very disappointed with Gregory though and decided that she didn't want to raise her daughter in the commune because she and Gregory had fallen out of love with one another.

The birth of Sasha gave Callie a new awareness and perspective on life. And too, she wanted more than the lifestyle and the rhetoric of the *Make Love and Peace Movement.*

So Callie made the decision to move from the commune but she needed to ask her parents for financial assistance until she could get on her feet.

They reluctantly agreed because they were still angry with her for dropping out of college.

But Callie's parents loaned her $5,000 and told her to make good use of the money.

That's when she found the apartment on Bermuda Street and quickly formed a few relationships with several men who became frequent visitors to her apartment.

The people in the complex were very curious and suspicious about what was going on with Callie and all those men.

One neighbor Grandma Swanson was known as the snoop in the neighborhood because she was always leaning out the window and watching to see what she could see going on in the lives of others. She even had the nerve to prop a chair near her window so when she gets tired of standing, she sits and watches neighbors for as long as she wishes.

People in the complex are always saying, "Nosy Old Grandma Swanson must be bored or something but she really needs to stop all that gossips about people and get a life!"

Her husband, Gary, died a few years ago and some neighbors believe it was her constant nagging and gossiping that sent him over the edge and drove him to Alzheimer's.

He had to be taken to Lawrence Senior Home because Grandma Swanson was unable to care for him.

However, once Gary moved to the Senior Home, he got better and lived another five years playing dominoes and cards with other residents.

Over the years, Callie had become painfully aware of the gossip about her but she was unaffected by what the neighbors were saying because she was doing what she felt she needed to do to make a good life for herself and her daughter.

Mostly, she had become accustomed to and enjoyed the free love and sharing that occurred when she lived in the commune in Belleview Village and she enjoyed being intimate with different men.

Yet, Callie did everything she could to protect Sasha from knowing what she was doing with her men friends.

Callie would often say, "Sasha, my friends are coming over to see me today because they want to make sure I'm doing okay so stay in your room."

But Sasha has some suspicion about what's really going on with her mother but she knows it is better to pretend to be in the dark about it.

Anyway, pretending not to know what's going on has always been a great coping mechanism for Sasha.

Callie caters to Sasha every whim by spending excessive amounts of money on new clothing, shoes and whatever Sasha desires. Yet, Sasha has the nerve to get angry with her mother when she doesn't get her way.

Sometimes, Callie wonders whether having Sasha as an only child was a mistake but it is too late to think about that now because Callie is way beyond her baby making years.

CHAPTER TWO

Sasha is now 21 years old and a freshman at the Claremont City College where she is studying Psychology. She also loves acting so she enrolled in a performance and arts class as well. She has been selected for the lead part in several plays and she has a very promising career if she decides to pursue it.

She chose Psychology as her major because she has a great sense of awareness about people and she possesses an uncanny ability to quickly analyze people by observing and interacting with them.

She believes that more often than not, people will always put their best foot forward for those who they wish to impress.

Yet, she has never had a steady boyfriend in her life because she hasn't met anyone that she feels is deserving of her love so she tends to date lots of boys.

She mostly believes that many of the boys are really immature and though she is intimate with some of them, she feels that many of them are unable to really satisfy her needs.

But all of that changed one Saturday afternoon when Sasha was shopping with her mother. Standing across from her was a tall and distinguished looking man who kept gazing at her.

Sasha flirted shamelessly with him by smiling and tossing her beautiful mane of hair and she knew just what she needed to do to hold his attention.

He was very tall with a muscular build and his salt and pepper hair complemented his nicely tanned skin. Standing about 6 feet tall, he looked very sexy in his white woven knit shirt and blue slacks.

Sasha kept gazing and smiling at him and he nearly dropped a package that he was holding because he was too busy looking at her.

It was clear that the man was much older than Sasha who could easily pass for a woman much older than 21.

Wondering how she would find a way to talk with him without her mother being suspicious, she told her mother that the man was a counselor at her school and she wanted to discuss her course plans for next semester.

Sasha introduced herself to John Belvedere. They made a little small talk and then John asked Sasha if she would be interested in going out sometimes.

Sasha replied, "Sure, how about tomorrow?"

John didn't know what to think. He had just met this young woman and yes, he had asked her out but he didn't expect such a ready, set, go response.

She wasn't even trying to play hard to get and that bothered John somewhat, yet, he wanted her in the worst way.

Sasha kept standing there looking at John and waiting for his response. He finally said, "Okay, I can manage that." "Where should I pick you up?"

"Oh, pick me up near the corner of Landau and Main Street around 8:00 a.m.," Sasha replied. She felt this would be better because her mother would be very upset if John were to show up at her door!

John agreed but he was somewhat nervous because he didn't really know Sasha's age but he reasoned that if she was in college, then she had to at least be over 18.

He was mesmerized with Sasha's good looks and he couldn't wait to see her again and for Sasha, tomorrow seemed like a lifetime. She was so excited she could hardly contain her excitement.

Sasha walked back over to the shoe department and her mother asked, "What were you talking to that man so long about?"

"Oh, that's John," Sasha replied. "We were just talking school stuff like I told you."

"John works in our school office."

Callie cocked her head to the side and placed her hand on her big wide hips and glared at Sasha as though she really didn't believe what she was telling her.

Callie told Sasha that she had observed her body language when she was talking to John and she said, "You didn't look like a student having a conversation about classes to me."

Sasha didn't respond and just kept looking for shoes and Callie let it go for now because she was too focused on finding the right shoes to go with the pretty blue dress she had just purchased.

The next day, John was parked in his car waiting at the corner of Landau Street near Sasha's school.

It was early so there weren't many students hanging out on the campus and that was good news for Sasha, who had lied to her mother by telling her that she had an early class that day.

Actually, that was one of the problems with Callie. She just took Sasha's word for everything and never really bothered to check her story even when she felt that something wasn't quite right about what she was telling her.

When Sasha neared the corner, John emerged from his shiny black sports car and he flashed his big broad smile and pearly white teeth.

As she walked closer, Sasha began to swing her hips from side to side and held her head up high as though she were performing in a fashion show or something. John obviously impressed by what he was seeing, winked at Sasha and then gave Sasha one Sterling rose and a peck on the cheek.

She smiled and looked John up and down while licking her lips and saying, "Damn, you look good!"

John kissed her once more on the cheek as she slid in on the buttery soft leather car seats.

John was dressed in a black pullover knit sweater that showed off every muscle in his arms and chest and his pants were nicely hung over his slim hips and nicely shaped behind.

As he smiled at her, she noticed that he had a large dimple in his chin and she was in love with his good looks.

Right away without hesitation, John took Sasha hands and with his deep sexy voice he said,

"I guess you know I want to make love to you."

He was like a school boy with his first big crush. Sasha knew that's what John wanted and so did she. She could see by the way that he was undressing her with his eyes that he was interested in more than talking with her.

But instead, John said, "Let's go for a ride and then we can see where things go."

"I don't want to push you into doing something that you don't really want to do."

Sasha touched his arm and said. "No, I want to."

As they drove aimlessly down a back road, John said, "So you introduced yourself to me as Sasha B so what is the B for?"

"Oh, the B is for Broadway which is my last

name but I have always been called Sasha B by my mother and others who are close to me."

"Oh, I see," said John. "Well, your name is very pretty and so are you!"

They both felt somewhat awkward because their obvious age difference gave them very little to talk about but talking was the last thing on their mind.

One thing was for certain; they were very hot for one another so any awkwardness they felt was overpowered by their mutual attraction to one another and their desire to make love.

John suggested they go somewhere where they wouldn't be disturbed and they could talk and have the privacy they both desired.

Sasha didn't ask questions but she assumed that John would be taking her to his home.

However, when they reached the Montclair Hotel rather than John's residence, Sasha knew right away that John was either married or he had a significant other.

She hadn't even thought to ask him if he was

married or not and John certainly didn't offer up that bit of information. But for the moment, it was unimportant to her.

John took Sasha by the hand and helped her from the car. They walked arm in arm into the hotel where they registered as husband and wife.

John was so anxious to get Sasha to their room to make love to her that he pushed the wrong elevator button and then they got off on the wrong floor. They both chuckled at their situation and then took the exit to a flight of stairs leading to the floor of their room.

When they reached their room, John quickly picked Sasha up and laid her on the bed and began undressing her and she allowed it.

As he undressed, Sasha kept her eyes glued to his beautiful body. She was pleased to see that John was very well endowed.

John began kissing her passionately and Sasha loved everything he was doing to her.

Then he turned her over to massage her back with a bottle of oil that he had removed from the pockets of his pants.

Sasha was totally caught up in the moment as John pulled her gently on top of him. It was like a thunderbolt had hit her and she could barely contain herself. She rubbed his muscular arms and kissed him passionately as they made love over and over again.

John had been with a lot of women and none had been so freely and without inhibitions as Sasha was with him.

Nothing was off limits because Sasha was quite comfortable with her body and she was not concerned with what John or any other man thought of her.

It was not as though she was going to bed with every man. She just wanted this man, at least on this day.

Sasha was very skilled in her lovemaking so John knew that she had been with other men but he was not concerned about it because he had been with many women.

John simply wanted to savor the moment and

the taste of Sasha.

They lay quietly on the bed for a while before speaking and John finally said, "That was nice, really nice, indeed."

Sasha being somewhat upset exclaimed, "Is that all you have to say?"

"Well, you were great!" John said, somewhat apologetically and feeling like he had done something wrong.

Sasha got up in haste, grabbed her clothing and ran towards the bathroom.

John jumped up behind her grabbing her from behind as she walked towards the bathroom door. "Let me go!" Sasha screamed.

"Oh, now you want me to let you go!" John exclaimed loudly.

"You sure weren't saying that a few minutes ago when you were all over me like an acrobat artist," John scoffed.

"Well, that was then and this is now!" Sasha shouted. "I'm going to take a shower and I would like for you to drop me off at school."

"Wasn't I good to you?" John questioned, "You were great but it's time for me to go!" Sasha snapped.

Sasha was not in the mood for a question and answer session with John. They both knew what they were getting into when they agreed to meet. Sasha got what she wanted from John and he got what he wanted from her so she didn't understand why he needed so much reassurance. She told John that she wanted to go ahead and take her shower so she can get to her class on time.

John sat at the end of the bed with his head in his hands. He couldn't believe that he had allowed this young woman to get next to him.

He wanted Sasha in the worst way but in reality, he knew that this was a one way street and he knew full well that Sasha was a big tease!

Too, he wondered how often she had trapped some foolish man into believing that she really wanted more than a one day fling.

Sasha emerged from her shower, looking refreshed and beautiful in her tight jeans that were rolled up at the ankles.

She wore black open toed platform shoes and a black and white polka dot blouse that was so tight her breasts look as though they would explode out of her blouse any minute.

She knew that one look at her and John would get turned on again. Sasha enjoys teasing men especially when she is aware that they want to be with her.

Sasha sat quietly while John completed showering and then he drove her back to school barely saying two words.

John let her out at the corner of Landau Street but not before asking to see her again. She told him, "No, this was a one-time thing." She then ran off across the campus as though nothing had happened between them.

Sasha had gotten John hooked on her and she had no concern about it. John knew it was due to the fact that she was so young.

And he couldn't afford to cause any trouble by trying to push a relationship with Sasha because he's married with two small children.

John and his wife, Ciara, have been married for ten years and they are very unhappy with one another but neither one wants to be the first to leave so there they sat, year after year in an environment of discontentment.

John's wife knows what's going on behind her back and although she is not cheating on him, it's not because she doesn't desire to do so. It's simply that she hasn't found anyone worthy of her love.

She and John have often discussed the differences between men and women and their views about love.

Ciara has confided to John on many occasions that she believes that most men don't care as much about loving a woman as they do about going to bed with them.

John always vehemently disagrees with her but in many ways he is the primary reason that Ciara holds such beliefs.

John was thinking about these conversations with his wife as he watched Sasha run across the campus for class.

He was thinking about how he had lusted after Sasha and she had gotten what she wanted from him and she didn't care that she had hurt his feelings.

But now he was wondering and thinking about Ciara and feeling pretty bad about how foolish he had been about Sasha.

Sasha made it just in time for her last class of the day. Her friend Drew wanted to know why she wasn't in an earlier class. Sasha just replied, "I had a doctor's appointment this morning."

Sasha wasn't worried about what anyone was thinking because she had already told her teacher that she would not be in her performance and arts class that morning so as far as she was concerned, she had covered herself and it was nobody's business where she had been that morning.

CHAPTER THREE

Ten Years Later

Sasha's encounter with John Belvedere, an older man, had a big impact on her life and it played a key role in the evolution of Sasha Amour, a high class Call Girl who easily makes $7,000 a month for the services she provides to her clients.

Sasha didn't get into this profession without thinking about it for a long time because she knew her mother wouldn't support her decision if she knew about it; however, Sasha was very bored with her life and desired some excitement.

Over the years, she would often think about how she had been so enthralled with John Belvedere, a man she hardly knew yet, she loved the excitement of being with him and enjoyed the rush she got when she saw how much he wanted her.

It made her feel powerful and it was a fantastic feeling of control!

Some of Sasha clients are famous or wealthy businessmen and others have been simply born with a silver spoon in their mouths.

Sasha lives in a penthouse in the Upper Montclair Haven District. Every day, she emerges from her penthouse dressed to the nines in 3" heels, and she wears beautiful custom designed dresses that fit her curvy body perfectly.

Sasha always has her famous black briefcase along with her which further makes her appear as though she is going off to work every morning; however, the briefcase contains a variety of adult toys that she utilizes on her clients.

Whenever she encounters someone outside of her business, she always identifies herself as a top executive for a large pharmaceutical company.

As she boards the subway daily to her business, men and women look at her in awe. It's hard not to notice her because she always looks stunning and she walks like she owns the world. All people can say about Sasha is, "You Go Girl!"

However, what people don't know is that Sasha is not working a traditional nine to five job because she spends her days and some evenings entertaining a variety of men at a High class Brothel called the Manteca Inn.

Although it is illegal to run a brothel in most parts of the country, Tula Chatman has been able to operate her business without any problems because many of her clients are wealthy and others hold high profile and influential positions and they too, are clients and regulars at the Manteca Inn.

The Manteca Inn is a $10 Million Mansion that is located in the secluded area of Winsville, a very lucrative area of Montclair that is surrounded by lavished Mansions owned by entertainers and wealthy businessmen.

Tula owns the Manteca Inn Estate which is a 30,000 square foot property, surrounded by a brick wall for privacy and situated on 6 beautiful acres.

The estate has 12 bedrooms; 14 bathrooms; a large kitchen and dining area; a grand theater; a fabulous tennis court; two swimming pools and there are other great amenities at the Mansion.

Fifteen years ago, Tula made millions as a high class Call Girl but she is up in age now and she no longer has the looks that once garnered her upwards of $9,000 a month in sales.

Each client of the Manteca is required to complete a questionnaire that has been designed specifically to extract personal information about the clients.

Once this information has been reviewed, clients are matched with a specific girl according to their response and the services purchased by them.

But clients are also allowed to make requests to be matched with a specific girl if they desire it.

There are ten beautiful girls on staff at the Mansion but Sasha Amour is the most requested by clients coming to the Manteca Inn.

Some of the girls make their home at the Manteca while others have their own homes and separate personal lives with their husbands and children.

The women who choose to live at the Manteca are charged $1000 a month for rent because they have access to everything they need at the Mansion.

Because of this, Tula is realizing a great deal of money from her business and from renting space to some of the girls.

Some husbands are aware of their wives profession and others do not have a clue but Tula is uninterested and uninvolved in her girls' personal lives.

The only thing Tula requires is that the girls are professional with all the clients and perform their job well!

Though there are ten Call Girls at the Manteca, the most popular girls are Sierra Knudsen, Sarah Swanson, Bolivia Laredo and Sasha Amour.

Sierra is 21 years old and studying to be an attorney but she needs the money that she is earning at the Manteca to pay for tuition so her plans are to save enough money from her work to attend school full time.

Sierra has a good business mind and she has also made some great investments in stocks and bonds which are reaping great returns for her.

Sarah Tinsdale is a single mother of two and she actually resides at the Manteca. She lives at the far end of the Mansion with her children ages 4 and 5. They are too young to know what's going on and besides her work take place in the upper bedrooms of the Mansion.

Sarah's goal is to have her own home and retire from the business in two years. By then, she hopes to have the money she needs to build a new home in an exclusive neighborhood where she can settle down with her children.

Bolivia Laredo is from South America and she is the one girl that Sasha views as any real competition because she is strikingly beautiful with long dark hair, olive skin and bluish green eyes.

The clients love her but not as much as Sasha because Sasha is considered to be the epitome of perfection by Tula's clients.

Sasha loves her days at the Manteca because she has a lot of clients and she is paid well to be with them.

However, Sasha is keeping a big secret from Madam Tula because Sasha is married to a high profile attorney, named Justin Taylor.

Justin has a law practice in New Jersey but he has no idea that his wife of seven years is a Call Girl. Like others, he believes that she is a Vice President for a pharmaceutical company.

Justin and Sasha met at a local bar one evening where they both were having drinks with other people; however, rather than concentrating on having a good time with his date, Melody Long, Justin couldn't keep his eyes off of Sasha.

Melody saw that Justin was preoccupied with another woman so she abruptly got up from their table, threw her drink at him and then ran off in a huff without eating any of the appetizers that Justin had ordered for them.

But the cruel thing about the situation was the fact that Justin didn't try to stop her from leaving.

And he was not bothered by the laughter generated by other patrons who had observed Melody throwing her drink on him.

He simply laughed with them and then proceeded to order another drink while finishing off the appetizers.

Justin gathered the courage to approach Sasha's table and introduced himself to Sasha and her date.

He gave them his business card and told them that he was out on the town to attract more business for his law firm.

As he talked, he was watching as Sasha smiled coyly at him. She obviously knew why Justin had really come to her table and she knew why his date had thrown her drink at him.

And though she was feeling good about being the cause of Melody's unhappiness, she couldn't let on to Justin that she was attracted to him.

All Justin could hope for was that Sasha would take the hint and give him a call. She did and as they say the rest is history.

CHAPTER FOUR

Sasha had become an exact replica of the many women she had grown accustomed to watching on her mother's adult tapes.

She often wondered why her mother even had the tapes until one day when Sasha came home early and caught her mother and one of her so called men friends' getting a nooner.

Sasha never let on to her mother that she had seen this episode. She had stood in the hallway of their home watching in envy as her mother and the man were caressing and making love to one another like two dogs in heat.

The roughness of their lovemaking turned Sasha on so much that she was captivated by it and she continued to watch quietly from the hallway.

Both Callie and her lover were caught up in their lovemaking and they were unaware that they had peering eyes on them.

It was the first time that Sasha had an actual orgasm without being touched; it was as though she had been the one laying on the bed not her mother.

From this point on, at every chance Sasha had she was watching one sex tape after another and she was easily turned on from watching them.

Pretty soon it was not enough to simply watch the tapes; she wanted to do what she was seeing the women and men doing to one another on the tapes.

So at the young age of 14, she became intimately involved with some of the boys in her neighborhood.

She always made them wear protection because she had often seen men wearing protection on the tapes but there were times when protection was not used. Sasha liked it both ways but she knew that she didn't want to get pregnant so she mostly practiced safe sex.

On occasions depending on how much she liked a boy, she would allow him to be intimate with her without using protection.

But now that she was a high class Call Girl, she would ask the men if they wanted bare skin or condoms. Bare skin cost the clients more because she felt it posed too much of a risk.

But Tula always insists that each girl has weekly physicals performed to ensure that they are clear of any sexual transmitted diseases.

Though Sasha enjoys being with her clients, she can turn her feelings on and off like water.

One of her clients, a billionaire from Europe, named Claude Dominic, visited Montclair City for the first time and discovered the Manteca Inn. Tula recommended Sasha as a good match for him and he wanted to spend the entire night with her.

However, Tula told Claude that he could only have an hour with Sasha because she had other clients to see that day.

But Claude told Tula that he would be willing to pay $10,000 to spend the night with Sasha so Tula quickly agreed to his request.

Claude Dominic was young and very handsome and all he wanted to do was talk. Sasha thought this was a weird request but if that was all he wanted to do then she was certainly fine with it.

As the night grew longer, and they continued to talk, Sasha leaned over and kissed Claude gently on his lips, he reciprocated and then Sasha began to work her magic on him.

Right in front of him, she took off the royal blue dress she was wearing and then pranced around the bed wearing absolutely nothing but 3 inch high heels.

Claude sat on the bed with his eyes affixed on her beautiful body and then dropped his pants and exposed the bright pink women panties he was wearing.

Sasha didn't know whether she should be freaked out or turned on by Claude. The truth is he did look foolish standing there in all his "pinkness" but he also looked sexy in a weird way.

Sasha could tell that Claude was well endowed by the way his panties clung to him. She called it a thunderbolt!

She grabbed at it and he snatched his panties off and threw her on the bed like a madman making love to her over and over again.

They went at it for an hour and Sasha wanted to keep going but it was Claude who was tired out and eventually, snoring over on the other side of the bed.

Sasha thought wow, this fool can't even last longer than an hour even with all my magic tricks; he is laid out dead to the world! No wonder he didn't want to do anything but talk.

Sasha showered, turned on the TV and watched a few adult movies while Claude continued to sleep. She chuckled to herself and after watching several tapes, she fell off to sleep.

In the morning, she awakens to see Claude is getting dressed to leave and he was standing there in his powder blue panties and a powder blue dress shirt.

Sasha couldn't help herself so she asked Claude, "What's with the panties?"

"I like the way they feel next to my skin," Claude responded. He was feeling a little self-conscious and thinking that he needed to provide a better response because he knew that a man wearing women's panties was probably a turn off for Sasha.

He told her that he started wearing women panties when he was about fourteen years old.

One day, when he was feeling bored, he went into his mother's bureau and removed a pair of her underwear and tried them on.

Liking the way the silk felt against his skin, he continued to wear them.

"You know how youngsters are with trying new things," John remarked.

"No, youngsters do other things," Sasha said. "It doesn't necessarily follow to me that a boy of fourteen would out of the blue want to wear his mother's underwear."

"Well, I did," John responded.

"And since that time, I've been stuck in the feeling I get from wearing something soft and silky next to my skin."

"Can't you get that same feeling from regular men's underwear?" Sasha questioned.

"No, it's not quite the same," Claude said, as he pulled his gray slacks up over his hips."

He was a great looking man but he was really not Sasha's type. There was a vulnerability about him that she saw as a weakness and although she had allowed him to make love to her, it was strictly business for Sasha.

That's all any of this was to Sasha and she was looking forward to being with her husband. She had told Justin that she was going to be away on a business trip and returning the following day.

Justin and Sasha have a mutual agreement never to phone one another while they are working.

They simply trust one another and don't see a need to check in with one another. If one doesn't come home, it is simply assumed that their business has intervened.

In many ways, Sasha and Justin have an open marriage without formally declaring it as such.

CHAPTER FIVE

Sasha had been thinking a lot lately about her profession and about what her mother would think of her if she knew what she was really doing for a living.

Sasha's mother was unaware of her profession and she also thought that Sasha was a Vice President for a pharmaceutical company. Worst, she often boasts about this to her friends!

But Sasha also held a truth about Callie that she had held for all the years she was growing up. She had long believed that her mother wasn't simply having friends over to her apartment. Callie was plain and simply providing intimate services to men and she was doing it out of her home.

But it took Sasha some time to come to this conclusion because she didn't want to believe this about her mother.

Sasha realized that her mother probably felt she had to be with numerous men because she had no obvious job skills.

Sasha knew the day that she came home early from school and found her mother with a man in her bed that something was amidst especially when she saw the man give her mother money.

She never told her mother about this incident and now her mother had gotten up in age and she was no longer able to have her love escapades.

Sasha provides for her mother by paying her rent and buying food for her but her mother would be devastated to discover that Sasha has followed in her footsteps.

Sasha is better at servicing men than her mother and she is making an average of $7,000 a month and sometimes more.

But she can't help but wonder about the toll her profession is taking on her body because she is intimate with at least 3 to 5 men daily.

Although Sasha often enjoys her interludes with other men, she truly sees this as a job.

But she couldn't do such a great job if she didn't enjoy being with different men. She likes being intimate with them and she is great at it!

Anytime a client comes to see Sasha, she reviews the selected services with the client. She also talks further with the client to find out if there are additional services that they would like to purchase.

One night, a client told her that he wanted her to bark like a dog during lovemaking because this would let him know how much she was enjoying him.

Sasha barked her behind off! She thought for the money he is paying me, I will beat my chest like a doggone gorilla if he wants me to! There is no shame in my game. No shame at all!

Despite this fact though, Sasha desperately wants to have a child that she can love and dote on but she knows that this is virtually impossible with her work schedule and that of her husband.

Additionally, she is living a lie and she doesn't want to bring a child into all her madness. At least not now because even though she loves her husband very much, they don't have a traditional marriage.

But Callie desires to be a grandmother so Sasha wonders how long she can lie to her mother about her profession.

At some point, Sasha knows that the truth will come out in one form or another and she is not prepared to deal with it. But for now, she is content letting her mother believe that she has a great executive job.

CHAPTER SIX

One evening when Sasha was preparing to see a client, a knock came at her door, it was Madam Tula who had received a phone call from a famous celebrity and he wanted to spend time with the most beautiful Call Girl that was available that night.

Madam Tula knew right away that Sasha would be the best girl for him so she went to tell Sasha about the celebrity client and Tula said she would reschedule Sasha's other client to another date or ask the client if he wanted to see another girl.

When the celebrity arrived, Sasha was shocked when she saw him because all her life, she had so admired the actor Darnell Obertree.

Darnell had been an example of everything that she wanted in her father but now she was confronted with the fact that the man in front of her, who she had so admired, was cheating on his beautiful wife Jennifer.

Nevertheless, Sasha had a job to do so as usual she began talking to him about the things he enjoyed to have done to him but at the same time she was thinking to herself, what a jerk you are because for Sasha it was a job and for Darnell it was pure lust.

As he started to talk more to her about doing what he wanted to do to her, Sasha was glad because it meant that she wouldn't have to work as hard because Darnell was willing to do it all.

All she would have to do is lie there and enjoy it but she was in for a surprise! As he began to kiss her mouth and her clit, he then suddenly sprung forward with his nice thunderbolt and asked her to massage it.

The thunderbolt is the name Sasha uses to describe men private parts because she feels this best describes the feeling she gets from it.

"What are you doing?" Sasha asked, as she tried to push him away from her mouth but he kept saying, "Come on baby, you know you like it!"

Sasha didn't want to admit it but it was really the way that he took control of her that she liked so despite the fact that she was disappointed at the fact that Darnell is a cheater, no other man had ever taken control of her the way Darnell was taking charge.

Although she would often talk to her clients about what they wanted her to do, Sasha would ultimately be the one to take charge and do whatever she wanted to do with them.

That was part of the thrill of being intimate with other men because she could dominate them and she is very knowledgeable about pleasing and satisfying men but this time was different.

Sasha began to tease Darnell with her tongue rolling back and forth over his thunderbolt, he was overcome with feelings of delight and she was enjoying making him feel good!

It was the first time in a long time that she had felt such overwhelming closeness with a man besides her husband.

The other time she felt this way was with John Belvedere with whom she had been intimate with only once.

She never confessed it to him, but John had made her feel so good that day that she knew she couldn't see him again because she didn't want John in control. Sasha wanted to be in control and she knew that if she allowed herself to feel anything for John, she would have been at the point of no return.

Sasha really doesn't understand what has caused her to be this way. Why is she so easy to have multiple partners? Why didn't it bother her? Why? She just didn't know but what she did know at this instance is that she liked the way she was feeling.

With each stroke Darnell was penetrating her deeper and deeper and they were both completely satisfied and she was in pure ecstasy.

She didn't know if it was because of who Darnell was or if she really liked him but at any rate, he was doing the job and at that moment, he was her only lover!

Sasha didn't know quite why she was feeling so good with this man because she had been turned off by the fact that she had admired him so long from afar and then disappointed that he was not what he had portrayed himself to be but at this moment, it didn't matter.

She felt very close to him but she knew that for Darnell it was only sex but she put all of that out of her mind for now and simply wanted to enjoy everything about him.

He rolled her over on her stomach bringing her to the biggest orgasm that she had ever experienced in her life!

Darnell was very skilled and even in his roughness which Sasha enjoyed so much, he was also gentle as he stroked the baby hair around her forehead, whispering how good she made him feel.

He said over and over again that her pussy was the best he had ever had and he screamed out, "I can't help it; girl, your stuff is good!"

Sasha was thrilled with his delight and she just kept caressing his arms and rubbing all over his body with pure delight.

At the end of their adventure, Darnell told Sasha that this was merely an encounter for him so "Don't go getting hung up on me," Darnell said sounding like he was some type of stud or something.

He could tell that Sasha wanted more from him but Darnell was just satisfying his desires and meeting his needs.

He was not about to give up everything he had with his wife. "That's the difference between men and women," he said to Sasha.

"We can remain detached and be with a woman and then go about our business as though nothing ever happened."

He was so cold! Gone was the tenderness she found in him previously. Sasha knew that this was the beginning of the end for her and that she could no longer play this role because she needed to try to build a solid foundation in her marriage to Justin.

CHAPTER SEVEN

It was a dreary night when a new client, known only as Steve, walked in and asked Sasha, "What's your pleasure?"

Sasha was a bit taken aback because this was generally her question to her clients so she didn't quite know what to say so she simply asked, "What do you mean?"

Steve quipped, "I mean I am here to grant you your fantasy."

"Well, you won't be able to grant it because there's only one of you," Sasha said smiling at Steve.

Steve liked the frankness of Sasha's response and he couldn't help but admire her because she knew what she wanted and she didn't mind making it known.

Sasha told Steve that her fantasy has always been to be with three men. She said, "I want one man to cuddle and caress my breasts, one to make love to my clit and one man at my feet.

If you can arrange this for me then you will have satisfied my fantasy."

Looking surprised by Sasha's response, Steve said, "Well, I will see what I can do for you. I have a couple of friends who I know like to have a good time and enjoy getting a little kinky so I will arrange this for you."

"What are we doing tonight?" Sasha asked. She was trying hard to change their conversation.

"I'm good with the traditional and whatever you desire to have done to you," Steve replied while smiling and gazing at Sasha.

"Sounds good!" Sasha agreed and she was relieved that she wouldn't have to work too hard because she wasn't really into it.

But Steve didn't want to jump into bed without knowing more about Sasha so he tried hard to get her to tell him more about herself but she was having none of it.

Sasha simply responded, "There's nothing to tell; I am just a big city girl trying to make a good living for myself."

"I don't ask anything from anyone and I don't expect anything except what I've earned, that is…"

"Don't you want to know a little about me?" Steve asked.

"Not really, I just want to do what I thought you came here to do."

"Just like that, no foreplay or anything?" Steve persisted because he was hoping that Sasha would be more forthcoming in his query of her.

"Well Steve, it's your pleasure today," Sasha said.

"Remember you have already paid for it!" Sasha exclaimed.

With that... Sasha got up from the bed and began to unbutton Steve's shirt. This was the opening act for what she was about to do to him because she began kissing and licking him all over his body.

He had never had anyone do this to him so he didn't know what to think but he had to admit that it was different.

Steve reciprocated and he became increasingly aroused by Sasha's reaction to what he was doing to her.

She suddenly climbed on top of Steve and rode him like she was riding for her life.

He couldn't control himself because he was so turned on by Sasha. With every stroke and movement, Steve moaned and groaned like a big bear. He kept saying over and over, "Please, don't let this feeling end!"

Afterwards, they lay in bed talking for a while and Steve said that he would definitely return the following Wednesday with the two friends that he had in mind for Sasha's fantasy.

Steve and Sasha took a shower together and then played around in the shower for a bit.

He left shortly thereafter and Sasha prepared to go home.

When she arrived home Justin was not home to greet her. This was the case most nights so they rarely saw one another but when they did, they were always caressing and making love throughout their home.

Justin was always buried knee deep in his legal business, defending white collar crime clients but Sasha's profession demanded a lot of her time as well.

The problem is that Justin has no idea that Sasha is a Call Girl and she shudders to think what Justin will do or how he will react if he finds out about her true profession.

But she knows that Justin has at least one other woman that he sees on the side but Sasha was getting a whole lot on the side so she wasn't really bothered by it.

Although love rarely if ever enters into a Call Girl's profession, Sasha was definitely getting her needs met on a daily basis.

She got ready for bed and to her surprise about an hour after she arrived home, Justin arrived home as well.

They chatted for a while and both told each other how much they miss and love one another.

Justin quickly showered and then returned to bed but Sasha had fallen asleep. He nudged her because he wanted to make love to her but Sasha was too tired so Justin let her be.

The next morning Sasha took a shower and made a cup of coffee for herself and Justin.

Like two ships passing in the night, Sasha and Justin were again preparing to go out without any lovemaking.

And there was a little tension on the part of Justin who was still annoyed that Sasha hadn't remained awake until he had completed showering.

Sasha leaned over the desk where Justin was working and she gave him a passionate kiss. He asked her how much time she had and she told him that she was running late but she would make time for him.

For the first time in a long time, she made love with her husband and they both fell in love all over again. She knew what he liked and he knew how to please her.

Justin tried to make up for lost time because he didn't know when he would have another opportunity to make love to Sasha.

It's not as though he didn't get any but no woman satisfied him like Sasha so anytime he could make love to his wife was a good time.

When their lovemaking was over they chatted a bit and then showered together. The lovemaking started up again but Sasha had an appointment with a client so she told Justin that she had to leave but she would be returning later that day.

She reapplied her makeup, got dressed and headed out the door. It was the same old routine and it was getting a little tiresome.

Sasha wasn't enjoying her encounters with other men as she once had because she was feeling more and guiltier about the secret she was keeping from Justin and her mother.

Even though she had formed some nice relationships with some very wealthy men, she knew that it would be an end to her marriage if Justin found out about her true profession.

She and Justin had mutually agreed that it would not be a deal breaker if one or both had another lover on the side.

Nevertheless, if Justin were aware that Sasha was a Call Girl and having sex with numerous men he wouldn't' tolerate it.

CHAPTER EIGHT

It's Wednesday morning again and as Sasha prepares to meet her clients for the day, she is reminded by Tula that Steve is coming and bringing along two of his friends.

She is somewhat amused and excited because she was partly kidding with Steve but secretly she has always had a desire to be with more than one man in what she calls a decent way.

So after she met with one client, she showered and prepared for Steve and the two guests he was bringing along with him.

Steve hadn't told Sasha anything about the men except that they enjoy doing Call Girls and both were very involved in these types of hook ups.

He did indicate that one was married but that was all Sasha knew about the men.

A knock came at the door and Sasha opened it to see Steve, another man and of all people her husband! They were both in shock and didn't know quite what to do but Justin blurted out abruptly, "I can't stay here and left."

Steve didn't know what was going on until Sasha told him that Justin was her husband and the other man just stood there looking like okay, so what do we do now?

Sasha swept it aside and said, "Let's finish what I started." "I said I wanted a threesome and we don't have that but let's go with it!"

How Sasha could sweep her feelings under the rug and not let anything rattle her was something that usually worked in her favor because by the time she reaches home, you can bet that she will have a feasible story for Justin and he can like it or not but she will stick to her story.

For now though, she is all about business and pleasure so she Steve and Leroy had a great time with Steve kissing her clit and Leroy played and fondled her breasts and other parts of her body for two hours.

As they switched positions and Leroy began kissing Sasha all over, they were so absorbed in the moment that none of them seem to be at all concerned about Justin.

Probably, because Steve and Leroy knew that Justin was no saint. He was having a variety of sexual encounters regularly with women in his office.

According to Steve, Justin is known all over the country as a player because he uses his business trips to fool around with different women.

In fact, Sasha knew Justin was seeing other women but not to the extent that she learned from Steve and Leroy.

Steve and Leroy were fed up with Justin's high and mighty attitude. The only reason Steve had even asked Justin to participate in the threesome is because he knew that he would be up for it.

"It is a case of who can out do the other in this situation," Sasha remarked calmly shaking her head at the entire situation.

Sasha decided that she would remain at the Manteca for the night because she wanted to give Justin a chance to cool down before she returns home.

When she thought about the whole situation, she didn't know what Justin was so angry about because they both knew the other was seeing other people but Sasha just was seeing a tad more than what Justin expected.

Nevertheless, from what Sasha heard from Steve and Leroy, Justin wasn't too much better than her so she was not worried about any ramification to their marriage but she still wanted to chill out overnight. She tried phoning Justin to tell him that she would be home the following day but despite the numerous calls she made to his office, he refused to take her call.

His secretary who was also was having an intimate relationship with him, according to Leroy and Steve, answered his phone and told Sasha that Justin was unavailable to take her call.

"Well, tell him I phoned and I will be late coming home!" Sasha remarked angrily.

Sasha was getting angrier by the minute over Justin' sanctimonious attitude.

When Sasha returned home, she found several packed boxes in the living room of their spectacular home but Justin as usual was nowhere to be found.

However, he left Sasha a note that indicated he would not be returning to their home. Just at that moment, several movers arrived to pick up the packed boxes that Justin left behind and Sasha was livid!

She and Justin had been married over seven years and although they didn't have a traditional or perfect marriage, they were in fact married and she knew that he loved her as much as she loved him but she was not going to beg him to stay.

CHAPTER NINE

Sasha phoned her mother and Callie abruptly hung up on her. Sasha phoned her back thinking there was a bad connection and her mother blurted out to her, "Tramp!"

Justin had phoned her mother and told her everything and Sasha felt he had no right to do this because she had always planned to tell her mother the truth about her profession in her own time.

But her mother was devastated and so was Sasha. She couldn't believe that Justin would stoop so low!

After all they had been through together and she had tolerated his relationships with other women and yet, he would betray her in this way.

But now, she had to keep her focus on patching things up with her mother.

Sasha wondered how she would explain to her mother that she had decided to be a Call Girl because she wanted to make a good life for both of them in the exact same way that Callie had done for the both of them so long ago.

This is what had made the entire situation so sad because Sasha had desired to be like her mother.

Even though she knew what her mother did for a living, she still admired her and was thankful for everything she had done for her.

In some ways, Sasha's profession was due to the fact that her father had decided not to be a part of her life.

She has always been looking for a father figure even in her husband Justin who had disappointed her and chosen to leave her rather than try to work things out with her.

Callie listened quietly as Sasha tried to explain and justify why she lied to her but in the end all of it didn't matter.

Callie's heart was broken! She loved Sasha and it wasn't even that she had chosen the profession that she had chosen as much as it was the fact that she lied about it.

What's worse, the many friends that Callie had bragged to about Sasha may have known the truth because there were a lot of nosy people in their old neighborhood.

Callie was embarrassed about this more than anything but she managed to say, "I Love You" to Sasha and hung up.

It was the last time Sasha would be able to talk with her mother, who fell dead from a heart attack that night.

Sasha made funeral arrangements and had her mother buried nicely. Justin didn't come to the funeral to support Sasha but he did send flowers.

He later tried phoning to give his condolences but Sasha wanted nothing more to do with him.

She realizes now that she had been married to a dream and that she had accepted Justin's behavior of seeing other women because she felt badly about her profession.

Now, she could see things more clearly and she realizes that they never really had a solid marriage. It was an arrangement that they both pretended to be a marriage.

Now that she no longer had her mother, there was nothing else to lie about. She needed to face her demons and figure out what really had caused her to choose the profession that she had chosen to enter.

She had blamed her mother and her missing father but she knows that everyone has a choice and she made hers.

It was time for her to be a real woman and take responsibility for the problems she created and she was now ready to do this. It would require her to go into the Manteca Inn for the last time to tell Tula that she is resigning from her job.

Tula had been at the funeral in support of Sasha so she understood how hard Sasha was taking her mother's death so she asked Sasha to take a couple of days to think about her decision.

However, Sasha indicated that this was the end for her and she would be moving on with her life in another area but she hadn't decided how she would do it.

She just knew that she needed to do something magnificent in her life where she could make a positive impact in others life.

She had always talked to other girls at the Manteca about her desire to do something to help women hold onto their men.

Sasha felt that sharing what she had learned from being in her profession would probably be helpful to many women.

Some of her clients had discussed personal aspects of their lives with her including what they desired to have done by their wives and it was not happening.

Yet, Sasha had not been able to hold onto her own man so she reasoned that she needed to do something else.

She didn't have to worry about money because she had a nice savings that she had accumulated from her profession and she also had her home because Justin had decided to relinquish any rights to it.

Knowing that she was in a good financial position made Sasha feel good and provided some comfort to her but she missed her mother terribly and desired to do something to honor her mother's memory.

It wouldn't erase all the years that she had lied to her mother but it would make her feel good that she was doing something worthwhile.

Sasha had learned a lot about running a business from Tula because there are some things that are applicable in all types of businesses and Sasha believed she had those skills.

She believed the best use of her experience would be a career where she could provide help and support to troubled teen girls.

She desired to help misguided girls stay on the right path and avoid looking for an easy way to make money.

She put up $150,000 of her own money to launch "On the Right Track," a school for misguided girls who are destined for trouble because of their poor choices.

Sasha believes strongly that although the Call Girl profession generally occurs in a safe environment, it is not a good choice for young girls.

Not that she criticized the profession because for the most part, Sasha had made a good living from it but she wanted girls that attended her school to realize and understand that they have more options in life and they don't merely have to settle for lying on their backs to make a good living.

Sasha developed and presented a business plan to the City of Montclair. The plan identified strategies and the advantages of her school program for the community.

She was able to show that by utilizing and assisting her financially with her program, the City would be able to reduce the cost that was currently incurred for locking up young girls for solicitation, drug use and other issues.

Ultimately, the City of Montclair liked Sasha's plan and decided to help fund the program because it was great for the community and the City.

But Sasha wasn't able to immediately shake her profession because when people found out that an ex-Call Girl was heading up the program, they protested and argued that Sasha was the last person that the City should partner with to help young girls.

Nevertheless, Sasha ultimately won the battle because she was able to quickly prove that her program was benefitting the community and saving money for the community.

One day a gentleman came to the school to enroll his daughter in the program. He was a single parent and according to him his daughter was out of control so he thought that Sasha would be able to provide him with the support he needed.

Immediately, there was a great attraction between Tony Leppo and Sasha but for now the focus needed to be on his daughter Tyler.

Tyler reminds Sasha of herself when she was her age because Sasha was doing some of the same things that Tyler is now doing including driving her father crazy. But in Sasha's case, she was giving grief to her mother.

Tony told Sasha that Tyler likes to stay out late and she enjoys showing off her beautiful body in skimpy outfits.

Tyler looks much older than her age so she is attracting the wrong element and mostly older men who mean her no good.

In fact, some of the Professors at her school behave as though they can't control themselves around Tyler.

Sasha knows exactly what to do and it starts with helping to raise Tyler's self-esteem.

Having a beautiful face and body doesn't mean that a person has self-worth so Sasha will work closely with Tyler on this need first and then work to determine what's really going on with inside.

There is an on-site psychologist that will help unearth some of the issues going on in all the girls' lives.

Some things are common with all of them including lack of self-esteem and mother or father issues that have not been resolved.

While all this is going on, Tony makes it a point to show up every day to support his daughter but Sasha is aware that part of the reason Tony is coming to the school every day is because he wants to see her.

At this point, no telephone numbers have been exchanged and Sasha prefers to keep it this way because her ultimate goal is to help Tony's daughter.

So far, the only thing going on between Sasha and Tony is an occasional smile. But sometimes when Tony drops Tyler off at the school, he makes it a point to thank Sasha for the work she is doing with Tyler.

Each program is six weeks long and some sessions are longer because each girl has different needs.

Tony is quietly hoping that everything goes well with his daughter because once Tyler completes the program; he is secretly planning a nice dinner with Sasha.

When the six weeks are up, Tyler graduates from the program with five other girls who were able to get their issues on the table and partially resolved.

They will require ongoing counseling before they can get to a good place but they will have access to the onsite psychologists to help them transition successfully out of the program.

The after support will involve helping the girls find jobs and helping them get through school including tutoring and any other support they require.

At the graduation, Tony approached Sasha to say thank you and he asked her out to dinner. Sasha told Tony that she didn't think that it was appropriate for her to have dinner with him because it will not look good to Tyler.

"Well, she is doing fine now and she is obeying the rules of the house," Tony responded.

"Yes, but trust me on this one, she isn't out of the woods yet, and I don't want her to suffer a setback," Sasha responded adamantly.

Tony agreed but he told Sasha that he hoped that she would give him a rain check.

"A rain check it is, when the time is right," Sasha agreed.

Over the next few months, Tyler established a close relationship with Sasha. The closeness occurred naturally due to Sasha's honesty about her past.

As a result, all of the girls felt comfortable sharing personal information about themselves with Sasha.

However, Sasha was still not sure if Tyler would understand or even accept her dating her father.

One day, after one of Tyler's tutoring sessions, Tyler told Sasha that she would love it if she would date her father.

Tyler had grown to like Sasha a lot and she is aware that her father has strong feelings for Sasha.

Initially, Tyler was angry about the attraction between Sasha and her father but she told Sasha that she now realizes that her father deserves to have someone special in his life because her mother had deserted them long ago.

Tyler explained that she had been fearful that if her father and Sasha were to get together, he would desert her as well. But she explained that she no longer have those feelings.

Sasha reassures Tyler that she would never do anything to come between Tyler and her father because her first priority is to provide Tyler and the other girls with the support they need to do well in school and in their life.

Sasha reasserts to Tyler that she will always put her welfare before any feelings that she has for her father.

The Call Girl profession sounds glamorous to Tyler so she wanted to know more why Sasha believes it to be a bad choice for girls.

Sasha felt it was necessary to provide Tyler with more personal information about her life as a Call Girl because she wanted her to fully understand the negative effects it had on her life as well as lying about it.

"Tyler, I think everyone deserves to choose the profession that is right for them but in my case, it was a desperate choice and an easy way out, Sasha said.

"It was way too easy for me to give into the lucrative money and I failed to understand how my profession would negatively affect others, like my Dear Mother."

"Shortly after finding out about me, she dropped dead from a heart attack because I had repeatedly lied to her. I never told her about my true profession. Simply, I misled my mother!"

"My husband also found out and in fact, he was the one to tell my mother about it."

"But it doesn't matter who told who what at this point but I could have made better choices and that's what I want for you and the other girls in the program."

"Don't take what you perceive to be the easy way out," Sasha cautioned. She wanted Tyler to understand that appearances aren't always what they appear to be.

"I still think you and my father would be great together, Tyler responded sounding so grown up. She was clearly not the same girl that had enrolled in the program six weeks ago.

Sasha didn't want to give Tyler false hopes so she simply said, "When and if the time is right for me and your father, it will happen on its own."

"In the meantime, I am happy to be living a life that is relatively simple and less complicated."

CHAPTER TEN

One evening Sasha received a phone call at home, the voice was familiar. It was her ex, Justin. He said, "I am sorry. I acted hastily and I miss you and I want to try again."

But Sasha wants nothing to do with Justin.

She realizes now that she accepted his crap because she felt that she had no choice. He made her feel as though she was lucky to have him and she didn't want him back.

Justin had heard from Steve that Sasha had opened a school for troubled girls and was doing well.

Steve had tried to take Sasha out a couple of times but she didn't want to start up a relationship with Steve because he was once a client of hers.

For this reason, she told Steve that he could phone her to catch up but anything other than that was out of the question.

Sasha was thinking about her conversation with Steve as she was talking with Justin who held the phone and didn't know quite what to say to Sasha. The silence between the two was deafening.

It was really over! No more thinking about him like she did after the initial divorce. She had cried nightly and couldn't get him out of her mind. She was truly over him and it was for the best. She simply said," goodbye Justin." "I wish you well!"

"Wait, I never got to apologize for telling your mother about you," Justin replied sheepishly.

Sasha said, "Well, it's too late now, Justin. Mother is dead! She had a bad heart for a long time and I've always known that she couldn't handle too much pressure or stress. I forgive you but please don't phone me again."

Justin hung up and Sasha was sad for a moment and then she quickly snapped out of it. She knows that she has a bright future ahead of her whether it is alone or with someone else.

Her take away from everything that has happened to her is that she needs to be honest and upfront at the beginning of any future relationships, especially, if she wants it to be a meaningful and sustaining one.

Months went by then out of the blue Tony Leppo called Sasha for a date. "I have given you the time you said you needed and now I would like to see where things will take us," Tony said.

"What do you think about going to the Montague Restaurant with me on Friday night? It's newly opened. I will pick you up about six and we will eat and see where things go from there."

Tony was cramming everything in at once because he wasn't about to give Sasha a chance to say no.

"Okay, sounds like a date." Sasha responded somewhat hesitantly. She just didn't know if it was still too soon for her to date but she was willing to take a chance on love again. She reasoned that it was only dinner so what harm could it do?

Tony picked Sasha up from her home promptly at 6:00 p.m. and he gave her two dozen long stemmed roses.

It had been a long time since a man had actually brought her roses or flowers of any kind and never two dozen of them. She was blown away by Tony's thoughtfulness.

Justin never brought flowers to Sasha because he told Sasha that flowers were for dead people.

She was also remembering that a client brought her roses once but that was not the same as having someone who you are beginning to care about bring you flowers.

Because of Tony's thoughtful gesture, Sasha believed the evening was already off to a great start.

At the restaurant, the evening was going well with a little small talk, an intimate booth for two and champagne. Sasha thought, what else could anyone ask for in a night out?

Later, Tony suggested going to a club down the street to take a spin around the dance floor. He said, "I am a little rusty at it but willing to try it if you want to do it."

Everything was going fine but as she and Tony were entering the club, a man put his hands on Sasha's shoulders and he said, "Don't I know you?"

Sasha looked puzzled by his question and then politely said, "I don't believe so."

"Oh, I know now," he said. "You're one of the girls from the Manteca Inn."

Sasha politely said, "Excuse me," and followed Tony to their seats. It was obvious that Tony was a little perturbed but Sasha said, "Oh, well! You know my background Tony, I have nothing to hide."

"I know but I just didn't expect to run into someone who knows you from that period of your life," Tony said.

"Listen Tony, I am still that person but I have chosen to focus my attention on a new life. No one ever escapes their past because it always catches up with you. The difference is I am not my past."

"I make no apologies. I was a Call Girl! It happened and in many ways it was good for me. I made a lot of money from that business and now I am able to help other young women including your daughter."

"I am not criticizing you for the profession you were in," Tony said. "I'm simply saying it would be easier if you had chosen another profession."

"Well, I didn't so I guess; this is where we say goodbye because from time to time, I am going to run into people who know me."

"It's inevitable, so I think the best thing for you to do is to take me home and there is no need to go any further with a relationship."

"I want to take things slow Sasha so can we at least start with that and see what happens."

"Tony, I can only agree to that if you can accept everything about me including my past and I am not sure you can handle my past."

"Maybe not but I really like you and I would like an opportunity to try."

"Can we at least start with that?" Tony questioned.

"Okay," Sasha agreed. "But don't get mad when I run into past clients. It is no different than running into an old boyfriend, husband or in your case, a wife. We all have a past."

"We all have been intimate with other people before meeting someone else. That's the way it goes! So either we are grownups about it or we simply call things off before we get too far along in our relationship."

"Look Sasha! I am crazy about you! I knew it

the very first day I saw you when I brought my daughter in to meet with you."

"I think you are fantastic and yes, I am willing to do whatever necessary to continue to see you but you will need to be patient with me as well."

"I am not perfect," Tony acknowledged.

"Neither am I and that's my point," Sasha remarked somewhat peeved by Tony's attitude about the incident with the stranger.

Tony took Sasha by the hand and they danced to a slow song from long ago.

As the music played on and on, Sasha felt tingles up and down her spine and it was obvious that Tony was getting a little turned on.

He wanted to be intimate with Sasha but he knew he needed to take his time, especially after the conversation they had just had with one another.

Tony and Sasha had a great time dancing the night away and when he took Sasha home, they shared a passionate kiss and then looked longingly into one another's eyes. Both wanting to do more than kiss but they knew that this was not the right time. They needed to take it slow so they both said good night and Tony went on his way.

CHAPTER ELEVEN

Tony and Sasha had been dating about two months when they both agreed that it was time to consummate their relationship. Those were Tony's exact words and it sounded so unromantic to Sasha but yet she was excited and anxious about making love with Tony.

They decided to go to the Remington Hotel, an upscale hotel in Montclair because they desired to make the night special.

Tony went ahead to get things set up for Sasha. He ordered rose petals from the hotel and had them strewn from the front door of the hotel room to the bedroom and bath.

He purchased a short black negligee for Sasha and ordered lobster tails, caviar and champagne. He also ordered strawberries and he had already stopped in town to purchase whip cream.

However, the whip cream was not for the strawberries. He wanted to take his hands and spread the whip cream all over Sasha's body and then lick it off.

But he wasn't certain if Sasha would be turned on or off by his whip cream fantasy.

When the knock came to the door, Tony opened it to see Sasha standing there in a long red dress that fit her body perfectly. The back of the dress was made of a sheer piece of material that gave the illusion of a bare back dress and it was done very tastefully.

The only thing Tony could say to her was, "You look sensational!"

Sasha said, "Thank you and so do you."

Tony was dressed in black slacks, black casual dress shoes and a white knit sweater. He was very handsome with thick black hair that was combed wild and sexy, and he had a thin mustache. He was gorgeous!

Tony pulled Sasha closer to him and kissed her. He told her that he had purchased something sexy for her to wear but he said, "Now I don't know if I want you to put it on because I love the way you look in that red dress."

Sasha asked to see the lingerie and then she began to take off her clothing because she desired to model the negligee for Tony.

She knew that Tony was getting turned on because the back of his neck appeared wet from perspiration.

He said, "Wait, don't put it on." He pulled Sasha close to him and practically threw her onto the bed.

As he lay on top of Sasha she could feel that he wanted her because he could not control himself. Tony started kissing Sasha all over her body and she was completely into him. She loved the way he was willing to take his time and not rush their lovemaking.

He was gentle when he should be and rough the way she liked it. Tony was definitely in the dominant role and Sasha was so carried away with him. He smelled and taste good as did she to him and they were like one.

Sasha had been afraid that the first time with Tony would be a disaster because that's what often happens the first time when one partner feels awkward or self-conscious but this was not the case with them.

They were two beautiful yet still imperfect people joining together in the most intimate way.

Later on as they lay together in one another's

arms, gazing into each other's eyes as two people in love often do, they talked about their future together.

Tony told Sasha that he could see himself marrying her in a few years when Tyler has gone away to college and out of the house.

Things were starting to move a little too fast for Sasha and there was one thing she knew for sure, if she and Tony were going to be together, she was not willing to put her life on hold until everything was settled with Tyler. She cared deeply for Tony and Tyler but not at the expense of her own future.

Nevertheless, she just let Tony talk and share his feelings and then Tony asked, "What are your thoughts about what I'm saying?"

Sasha said, "Honestly, it's way too early for us to be having this conversation because I don't know how I feel at this point. I know I care deeply for you but I can't say that I am in love with you because I still have some unsettle feelings from my previous marriage. I mean I am no longer in love with Justin but we were together seven years so I simply don't want to rush into another relationship."

"Let's enjoy one another for now, take things slow and see how it goes. Let's not ruin a good thing! "

Tony responded disappointed, "Well, I thought you felt the way about me that I do about you."

"I do, that's the scary part!"

"What's scary about it?"

"I don't want either of us to do something we will regret."

"For instance, I want a child and you already have Tyler. How do you feel about having another child?"

"Honestly, I hadn't given it much thought because it has been me and Tyler for so long. Well, that's my point."

"It doesn't sound as if you're interested in having any more children."

"Well, maybe. I don't know."

"If I was the right woman for you, you would

know!" Sasha exclaimed.

"Wait a minute; you are the right woman for me and the only one for me."

"That's your lust talking," Sasha remarked.

"My lust?"

"It's me, Tony Leppo, being of sound mind and body saying, I Love You." Then Tony leaned closer to kiss Sasha's ruby red lips."

Sasha took a deep breath as though she had just been asleep and awakened by her Prince Charming.

She told Tony that she believed that they should take it one day at a time with no great expectations.

And Sasha didn't want to be part of a relationship where there was not total honesty between them and she wanted to be in a monogamous relationship with him.

"There are to be no third parties," Sasha said emphatically!

"I can live with that because the only woman I

want is you."

"Look Tony, I have lived the other life and I know that is not the way I want to live my life. That's what I know for sure, my past is my past and it is behind me."

"Good, stop talking because I want to enjoy you right now Sasha. We won't talk any more about tomorrow promises and tomorrow what ifs. Let's just make this thing work!" Tony exclaimed. He was excited about the future with Sasha.

Sasha agreed and they tried to salvage the food that Tony had ordered and delivered to the room.

The lobster was cold but still quite good and the champagne and strawberries were magnificent. This was the perfect ending to a night full of love and enchantment. It was like a fairytale and Sasha didn't want to wake up.

CHAPTER TWELVE

Tony and Sasha have been dating for six months and everything is going great for them. They are together at least four times a week and they enjoy their intimate time together.

They are both very committed to one another however; Tony was about to get a big surprise!

Prior to swearing his love and commitment to Sasha, Tony had been dating a young woman named Cecily Long.

His daughter, Tyler was unaware that he was seeing Cecily because Tony would drive to Cecily's home in Sunset City to see her. Sunset City is a small town right outside of New York City.

Tony and Cecily dated one another for a while but they had mutually decided to go their separate ways because Cecily cared more for Tony than he did for her and Tony told her that was not going to change.

One day, Cecily phoned Tony at his job to let him know that she was eight months pregnant and she was due to deliver his baby in about four weeks. Tony was flabbergasted by Cecily's announcement.

"Are you crazy?" Tony questioned.

"That cannot be my baby!"

"I haven't had sex with you since we broke up over 8 months ago."

"You're right, and that's why I am phoning you!" Cecily said fuming about Tony's reaction.

"At first, I considered giving the baby up for adoption but I decided to keep the baby and raise it myself without telling you."

"However, I decided that it took two to make this baby and my baby deserves to know his or her father."

"Why you little, floosy!" Tony yelled out loud while holding the phone away from his ears.

"Floosy, you didn't think I was a floosy when you were making love to me every Friday night for four months straight," Cecily fumed.

"I told you that I wanted sex only and you told me that you were taking birth control pills, Tony argued.

"I was on the pills but something went wrong."

"That's right something did go wrong and that was me getting involved with you in the first place." Tony was more than upset with Cecily but he knew that he could have ensured that Cecily didn't get pregnant by wearing a condom.

But that fact didn't keep him from being angry and he tried to bargain with Cecily.

"What do I need to do to make this problem go away?" "How much money do you want?"

Tony was trying to resolve the problem and he thought if he offered money to Cecily, she would both give the baby up for adoption and leave him alone.

"I don't want anything from you Tony."

"I am simply letting you know that you are about to be a father."

"Well, Tony said, I'm already a father to my daughter Tyler and she is all I can handle right now."

"I don't want another child."

Cecily told Tony that she had been dining at the Montague Restaurant in Montclair a few weeks ago and she saw him being very cozy with a woman."

"Is that why you decided to contact me, Cecily?"

"Is that what this is about?" Tony asked.

"You are jealous of seeing me with another woman."

"No, but seeing you with her, made me realize that I needed to let you know what's going on with me and your child." Cecily answered.

"Stop saying my child because that is not my child that you are carrying!"

"I want proof because I will certainly not take your word for it!" "I won't a blood test."

Cecily told Tony that she understood why he was so upset but she told him that she was sure the baby was his because she stopped seeing other men when she started dating him because he had asked her to.

Tony realized that it was too late to second guess what Cecily was telling him because he knew that the bottom line is that he could very well be the father of Cecily's baby. His concern though was how he would break the news to his daughter and Sasha.

Although Tony tried to be rational about being the father of Cecily's unborn child, he still argued with her insisting that she should have talked with him before deciding to keep the baby.

But nothing he said made a difference to Cecily because there was one thing for certain, she couldn't undue the pregnancy.

The baby was going to be born with or without Tony's agreement.

Tony wanted to meet with Cecily in person so he asked Cecily if they could meet at her home the following day and she agreed to see him but she warned Tony that she would not give her baby up for adoption and she told him if that was what he was hoping for he was wasting his time.

Tony was aware that he would not get anywhere with Cecily unless he had a clear head so that he could make good decisions about Cecily and the baby.

When Tony hung up from talking with Cecily, he knew that he needed to go home for the day because he wouldn't be able to focus on his job. Tony is a Senior Engineer for a large engineering company and it requires him to be meticulous and focused.

So John left for the day and headed home where he saw Tyler in her room studying. He chatted with her for a few minutes and then said to her, "I hope you know how much I love you."

Tyler smiled at her Dad and then got up from her chair and gave him a big hug.

Tony went upstairs to bed but he couldn't sleep because he wondered what and how he would tell Sasha about Cecily and the baby.

Sasha and Tony had both agreed to leave the past in the past but Tony hadn't counted on Cecily's big surprise.

Also, he had been so uncertain about having a baby with Sasha so he knew that she would be hurt if not devastated by his news. Tony reasoned that he had to find a way to make it right for everyone.

The next day he drove to Sunset City without having a chance to tell Tyler he was leaving.

Tyler was still sleeping and she looked peaceful when Tony looked in on her so he saw no cause to awaken her.

While driving, Tony was trying to analyze the entire situation with Cecily to determine what did it all mean, he knew no matter what, someone would be terribly hurt by his actions but then he thought I did not set out to hurt anyone. Tony believed that he was clear with Cecily about his intentions so there shouldn't be any expectations on Cecily's part except for him to provide for the baby.

On the other hand, he was thinking that Sasha would probably never see him again when he tells her about Cecily and the baby.

When Tony reached Sunset City, he phoned Cecily to let her know he was about ten minutes away.

Cecily didn't answer the phone so Tony went to her home where he saw a familiar face leaving Cecily's home. It was Justin Taylor, Sasha's ex.

Tony wondered what Justin was up to and what was going on with Cecily and Justin?

Tony recognized Justin because he had seen him on the News a while back because he was the lead prosecuting attorney and responsible for the conviction of three high ranking executives who embezzled millions from their company.

Tony watched Justin pull off in his red sports

car and then rung Cecily's door bell. Cecily quickly answered probably thinking it was Justin.

She looked startled when she saw Tony and asked him how long he had been outside.

Tony said angrily, "Long enough to see you with Justin Taylor." "What's going on Cecily?"

"Nothing is going on?"

"Whose baby are you carrying?"

"Are you pregnant with Justin's baby because I am convinced now that you are not pregnant with my baby?" Tony said.

Cecily broke down crying and then said, "Okay, the baby is not yours."

"Justin has been scheming to get Sasha back ever since he found out that she was dating you and he even hired a private detective to spy on you and his ex-wife."

"I use to date Justin but the baby is not his baby."

"And it's not mine, right!"

"No, Tony the baby is not yours."

"Justin told me to say it was yours so that his

ex-wife would find out and leave you."

"He said Sasha would never stay with you if she found out you were having a baby with another woman."

"So let me understand this; you were going to set me up that way!"

"Well Tony, look how you reacted to me when I told you that you were the father. Your response was horrible!"

"How much was he Justin is offering to pay you?"

"He was going to pay me $50,000."

"So who is the father of your baby, Cecily?"

"Dante Moore is the father of my baby."

"We have dated off and on for a long time.

"We met in college and he lives in Montclair and is a very wealthy businessman running several high end restaurants including the Montague."

"Oh, so that's why you were there?"

"No, that's not why I was there."

"I told you Justin was spying on you and Sasha so he knew your every move and where you would be."

"He asked me to go to the Montague to spy on you as well and that's when I first saw you with Justin's wife."

"She is his ex-wife!"

"Whatever Tony!"

"Tony, I am so sorry about all of this, I never wanted to hurt you but he offered me all of this money."

Tony was in disbelief and so angry he thought he better leave before he did something he would regret. He stormed out of Cecily's home obviously angered by the lies conjured up by Sasha's ex.

However, Tony was relieved that he was not the father of Cecily's baby and even more relieved that he wouldn't have to say anything to Tyler.

However, he did need to talk to Sasha immediately and he would need to tell her everything.

Tony phoned Sasha and she was very short with him but then Sasha said, "Justin phoned me to tell me that you are keeping a secret from me and he wanted to come over to tell me all about it."

"However, I told Justin that I would talk to you about whatever the secret is so I will see you at my home about 6 p.m."

"Okay, Sweets!"

"I will see you then but I can tell you not to worry because it's one big lie created by Justin."

"Okay, now you have my attention!" Sasha exclaimed.

Justin had betrayed Sasha by telling her mother about Sasha's true profession so she could only imagine what Justin had done to Tony.

Still Sasha was anxious to talk with Tony in person plus she was dying to have him make love to her again but she couldn't allow her mind to think about this right now.

Tony arrived promptly at Sasha's home and then suggested that they go out to a restaurant so they could talk with calm heads because he thought that this would be a better strategy but Sasha didn't want to go to a restaurant to talk.

She believed whatever Tony had to tell her was pretty serious because he appeared to be trying to do everything to avoid telling her about his secret.

Tony decided to just come out with it so he said, "First let me say it again, I love you very much!" "I have never felt what I feel with you with any other woman including my wife."

"Sasha, when you and I were last together you emphatically said that our past partners were the past and we would leave it there so I saw no need to provide you with intimate details on every woman I have had in my life."

"But when I first met you, I was seeing another woman, it was never serious but it was an intimate relationship and that's all it was for me."

"Justin found out that I had been dating her and knowing that she was pregnant with another's man's baby he convinced her to lie and tell me that the baby was mine."

"He went so far as to spy on you and me and he offered Cecily $50,000 to say the baby was mine."

Sasha had let Tony have his say without interrupting him but she couldn't believe what she was hearing.

"What the heck are you talking about?" Sasha groaned.

"So you are telling me that you were going with me and another woman?"

"No Sasha, I stopped seeing her a month after I met you because I did not want to ruin any chance of getting with you."

"Tony, I have been around the block a few times but I never saw this coming!"

"What Justin did was wrong, very wrong but you got up on your high and mighty when the man tapped me on the shoulders at the dance club and all along you were seeing someone else."

"No, that was way before we got serious about one another."

"News flash Tony, I was always serious about you! I need time to think about this. It's too important to me."

Tony reached out for Sasha and she pulled away. She was dying inside because her body ached for him but she needed time to think.

She had been married to one fool and she sure as heck didn't want another disappointment. She told Tony she wanted to chill their relationship for a couple of weeks and then they both could see if they were simply a match physically or did they truly love one another.

Sasha had to be sure. Tony pulled Sasha closer to him and she tried hard to resist him but she couldn't so they kissed passionately. They both wanted each other badly but Sasha told Tony to leave.

Sasha immediately phoned Justin to tell him that he was a cruel and pathetic man. Justin continues to swear his love for Sasha but she wasn't in the mood to hear his crap because she was outraged by what he had done to Tony and to her.

To make matters worse, he had the nerve to tell Sasha that he did it for her because he wanted to show her that no one is without baggage and secrets.

"You're crazy Justin."

"But I love you Sasha."

"No, Sasha said, you love you and I want nothing more to do with you."

"Don't phone don't write, don't bother me, Just leave me alone, Justin!"

"Okay, if that's what you want but you mean you don't want to feel me inside you like you use to love to do when we were married?"

"Remember how you called it your thunderbolt."

"I call all of them thunderbolt so don't go acting like you're some kind of stud or something," Sasha was angered by Justin failure to realize the seriousness of what he had done to her and Tony.

"Sasha you really hurt my feelings with that last comment."

"Well, leave me alone, Justin."

"Okay, if that's the way you want it but I will give you one more chance to change your mind otherwise someone else will have me all to themselves."

"I doubt that but have a nice life, Justin."

"Goodbye Justin!"

When Sasha hung up from talking, and hollering at Justin, she was very clear about what she needed to do in her life and it didn't include Justin or Tony.

She knew now that she loved Tony but he was too willing to buy his way out of the problem he had with Cecily.

Cecily had shared that bit of information with Justin after her confrontation with Tony.

In a lot of ways, Tony was no better than Justin except that he was a better lover but even that was not enough for Sasha.

It wasn't so much that he knew how to use his equipment so well but Tony knew how to romance the mind and sometimes that is a bigger turn on than the actual lovemaking itself.

But Sasha knew that she needed to be strong and she needed to move on at least for now so that she could get a clear mind about what she wanted to do with the rest of her life.

CHAPTER THIRTEEN

Weeks passed and Sasha hadn't heard from Tony. He actually hadn't done anything to make Sasha feel that he truly loved her.

And she wasn't about to phone him because Tony was the one who was willing to deceive Sasha and go to great lengths to keep her from finding out about his past girlfriend and her pregnancy.

However, one day while shopping in town, Sasha happened to see Tony at a sidewalk café' having lunch with another woman.

Sasha made it a point to walk pass their table so Tony could see her but he turned his head away as though she didn't exist.

Sasha couldn't believe what she was seeing but it was really what she needed because it proved that when someone tells you they love you, it is important to remember that those are simply words.

Sasha knew that this was the final confirmation she need to move on and she knew she needed to take control of her feelings for Tony and get her life back on track.

Sasha believed that the way to do this was to close her school for a few weeks so that she could take a vacation to clear her mind before doing something too drastic.

She decided she would vacation in San Antonio, Texas because she had visited there once with Justin and she simply loved it.

At first, she was concerned that this may not be a good idea because she didn't want to be anywhere or near anyone that reminded her of

Justin but she decided to take the trip to San Antonio.

In order to avoid checking into a hotel, she found a time share that she was able to rent for a few months.

She wasn't sure whether she would be in San Antonio for one month or three months but at least she had an option if she liked the location of the timeshare and needed more time to regroup.

Sasha moved into a condominium complex and found that people were very friendly but they didn't impose on Sasha's privacy.

However, not long after Sasha moved into the condo, she was approached by Antonio Ballentine. Antonio didn't have a lot of money but he owned a small trucking company in San Antonio and made a modest income from it.

He had seen Sasha when she first moved in and couldn't wait to meet her, so he rang her doorbell one evening with an apple pie and vanilla ice cream in hand.

No flowers, just a nice practical housewarming gift from a man, no less. Sasha was impressed.

The first thing that ran across the Sasha's mind was the fact that she had come to San Antonio to get away from two men because she wanted to clear her mind and here she was already being wooed by another man.

She thought, okay, the ice cream and pie are simply a nice gesture so what harm could come from it?"

Sasha could see that Antonio was a younger man but nevertheless, she wasn't intimidated or concerned about his age.

Antonio didn't waste any time. Right away he wanted to know all about Sasha. She told him a few things about herself but she didn't discuss her past job as a Call Girl with him.

Too, she didn't discuss Justin and Tony with Antonio because she didn't feel it was necessary because despite her instant attraction to Antonio, she didn't believe they would have a relationship.

However, the more she looked at Antonio as he talked freely and openly, Sasha hung on his every word because he was a very warm and seemingly sincere man and he was very handsome!

Sasha instantly thought this man is Hot! Antonio made his move by first taking a spoon of ice cream and then leaned over to kiss Sasha. She tried to pull back but she couldn't resist him.

His cold tongue felt good as he kissed her passionately! It was the most sensational kiss she had ever experienced.

Then he cut a piece of pie and fed her a tiny piece of it. He then pulled a small bottle of champagne from the inside of his jacket and asked Sasha if she had any champagne glasses, she did so he poured them both a glass as they gazed into one another's eyes.

Antonio was making his move on Sasha. She tried to pull away from him but he said, "What are you fighting me for because I know you are attracted to me. I can feel it and I am attracted to you so what is keeping you from giving yourself to me and I mean really giving me all of you right now!"

Antonio moved closer to Sasha and as she reached out to caress him, his body and hers radiated intensive heat.

Sasha wanted him to take control and as though he could read her mind, Antonio gently pushed Sasha back onto the sofa and she didn't fight him.

She began to unbutton her blouse and she snatched his shirt off because she was hot for him.

For a moment, Antonio laid on top of Sasha rubbing her shoulders, and playing with her hair.

Sasha was so turned on and she wanted Antonio to do more than play in her hair. She took his hands and guided them down her body over her nipples and onto what she calls her furry precious.

Then he suddenly got up and took another spoon of ice cream and then began kissing her clit. At first it felt cold but then it was the most sensational feeling and she could do nothing but let him take charge and continue to do all his magic tricks with the ice cream and apple pie.

It was as though the ice cream and pie became his props that he used to pleasure her in every way!

Sasha rubbed Antonio thighs and all over his body and he held her close to him.

It is not as though Sasha didn't have experience in being intimate with someone she hardly knew but this time was different so even though she was enjoying what Antonio was doing, she whispered softly, "Get up."

But Antonio kept doing what he was doing and Sasha was having a difficult time convincing herself that she really wanted him to get up!

The more Antonio kissed her and pulled her hair as he rubbed her body gently, the more difficult she found it so Sasha relented and gave in telling Antonio that he could do whatever he desired! She loved the fact that Antonio was an exceptional lover and he knew how to pleasure a woman and she was hypnotized by his rugged good looks.

He had an eagle tattoo on his back that was very sexy and the wings of the eagle expanded across his shoulder blades. It looked menacing and sexy at the same time. It was inscribed with the words, "Soar like an Eagle."

But it was Antonio's simple approach that had enticed Sasha. She thought to herself, what kind of man brings ice cream and apple pie to a woman he wants to seduce? She didn't know but it was something about this gift that made Antonio unbelievable attractive, innocent and sweet and Sasha was hooked!

When Sasha and Antonio came up for air which seems to be after hours of lovemaking, they talked more about what they desired out of life and what they wanted from one another, if anything.

Sasha didn't know how long she would be staying in San Antonio but she liked Antonio so she decided that she would continue to see him but she had no expectations for the relationship.

She simply liked him and he seemed to like her so nothing else was required.

After all she had already left Montclair to get away to clear her mind so her goal was to filter through all the things that was happening in her life to determine what she wanted to do.

One thing for sure, the things that were once important to her were no longer important. She didn't need anyone with a lot of money because she was very wealthy and she could take care of herself.

She wanted someone decent with good qualities and most of all he had to love her unconditionally.

She didn't know if Antonio was the perfect fit for her or this could be a one time thing with nothing else going on but if that were the case, Sasha was okay with it.

Sasha was thinking about the fact that men do it all the time and they are still considered men but when women have one night stands they are considered to be tramps.

Sasha was not concerned about this because had needs and she was meeting them. Tomorrow was another day.

CHAPTER FOURTEEN

A month later, Sasha loves every aspect of her life. She is enjoying being with Antonio and for the first time she is taking time to be alone with herself.

Antonio comes around about once a week because that's the way Sasha wants it. She doesn't want to be looking at Antonio on a daily basis because she understands now that her primary problem is that she has always felt the need to have a man in her life.

Perhaps, this has to do with the fact that her father was not in her life; she really didn't know the real reason but she wanted to break out of this and be whole with or without a man. She liked Antonio though because he didn't make any demands on her nor did he impose on the times that she wanted for herself.

He was busy with business most of the time and he worked long hours. Often he would develop terrible headaches because he worked too hard trying to ensure that his business continues to be profitable.

He never talks about money with Sasha but he has admitted to Sasha that he has a son from a previous relationship.

But mostly, they talk about the things that are in the here and now and they don't talk about their past relationships because they are just enjoying one another and still taking it one day at a time.

However, Sasha hasn't been feeling as well as she usually does and she feels that all the turmoil that she has experienced with the death of her dear mother, her job and her relationships with Justin and Tony have all caught up with her.

She knows that although she has been having a good time, she can't leave the school in Montclair in limbo. She has to make some definite decisions within a few weeks.

The on-site psychologist for the school has agreed to stay on regardless of whether or not Sasha decides to return to the school but the question is who will take over Sasha's role. Sasha is great in her counseling role because she identifies so well with the girls and that is mostly attributed to her past experiences.

When she phoned Tula before leaving Montclair, Tula gave her the name of someone who would be a good choice to lead the school if Sasha decides not to return.

Sasha's first order of business is to make contact with Bretta Moore to find out her availability and learn more about her experience in dealing with troubled teen girls.

In the meantime, Sasha has scheduled a doctor's appointment to find out why she isn't feeling quite up to par. She has an appointment today and hopes that she will be able to get something to help her feel more like her old self.

The doctor sees her and after examining her and performing a few tests, Dr. Ratio tells Sasha that she is about 12 weeks pregnant.

Sasha is beleaguered because she has only been in San Antonio about two months so if she is 12 weeks the baby is definitely not Antonio.

But she wonders who baby is it because she had been intimate with clients, Justin and Tony.

Sasha was devastated! She wants a baby badly but she wants it with someone she really cares about and that is Antonio.

She wondered what she should do now because Antonio certainly wouldn't want to be involved with her if he found out that she was pregnant with another man's child.

Nevertheless, Sasha knew that she had to tell Antonio the whole truth about her life. She felt she owed him that much because he has been so open with her about himself and she was beginning to fall for him.

Sasha phoned Antonio at his job and asked if he wanted to come over for dinner.

He said, "Sure, I always want to see you," and showed up promptly at 6:00 p.m.

Sasha decided not to cook because she didn't feel like it so she ordered several of Antonio's favorite dishes from a local restaurant and she set a beautiful table.

When Antonio arrived, he could tell that there was something else on Sasha's mind. She poured him a glass of wine but she didn't pour a glass for herself. As he sipped on the wine Sasha said, "You know I like you a lot Antonio and I haven't told you much about myself because I wasn't sure how our relationship would develop."

"However, I received some news today and I need to share my life with you because it affects you."

Sensing the seriousness in Sasha's voice, Antonio jokingly said, "I'm all ears, baby!"

"First let me tell you that I am a former Call Girl and worked at the Manteca Inn in Montclair."

Antonio repeated, "A Call Girl" as though he was trying to understand that he was hearing her correctly.

"Yes, I worked at it for several years before leaving."

"I was married at the time and my husband had no idea that I was a Call Girl. He is an attorney in New Jersey."

"Wow, I can't believe this about you. You are so nice and so classy!"

"Well, Sasha said, there's more!"

"After my husband found out about my profession he told my mother and she later died from a heart attack, most probably from the shock of hearing I was a Call Girl".

"My husband and I are divorced but he still tries to get me to come back to him."

"In the meantime, I started dating another man who is nice but he disappointed me so I decided to leave Montclair for a vacation here in San Antonio."

"I wanted to have an opportunity to think clearly about what I want to do with the rest of my life because I also operated a school for troubled teens."

"So, when I came to San Antonio, it was not my intentions to get involved with anyone and then you appeared and I really, really like you!"

Antonio didn't know what to say and then Sasha said, "I'm not finished, there's more!"

"I saw the doctors today and I was told that I am twelve weeks pregnant."

"Well Sasha, we know it is not my baby since you have only been here about two months."

"That's right Antonio but I wanted you to know about it!"

"I am so sorry Antonio."

"Don't be sorry, Sasha!"

"I am glad you finally told me the truth but I

wish you had told me sooner."

"Would it have made that much difference to you?" Sasha asked.

"Yes, Sasha, it probably would have but that's not important now."

"What are you going to do?" Antonio asked not knowing what to say to her.

"I don't know because the baby could be my husband's or Tony, the one I saw before ending our relationship and coming to San Antonio"

Antonio appeared to have lost his appetite but made polite conversation. Then he suddenly, looked up at Sasha and asked, "Have you considered remaining in San Antonio?"

She had but she just didn't know what she would do now.

Antonio suddenly blurted out, "Do you want to marry me?"

"Married, are you serious?" Sasha asked.

"Why would you want to marry me after all I just told you?"

"I love you Sasha!"

"You make my life exciting and I have a difficult time whenever I am away from you too long."

"Sasha, we are so good together and I'm not just talking about our lovemaking."

"I don't care whose baby you are carrying."

"We can make it work."

"You're telling me that you don't care about the fact that I was a Call Girl and with other men."

"No because I have been with other women so it doesn't matter to me."

"What matters to me is who you are right now today, and that is, you're the best thing that has happened to me in a long time." Antonio said while gazing into Sasha's beautiful eyes.

"So, what do you say?"

"Will you consider marrying me, Sasha?"

"Let me think about it because I have a lot of loose ends to tie up back home."

"Well, we can go back there together." Antonio responded.

"We could but I want to think without the

pressure of knowing that you are with me expecting an answer."

"Oh, okay, well I can be patient just let me know what you want to do."

"Antonio, you know I could decide to stay in Montclair and just have the baby and raise it on my own," Sasha said.

"I know that's why I want to come with you but you're right, you need to make your own decisions."

"I support whatever you want to do and I want to keep seeing you so I will be up front with you so you know that I am not planning on going anywhere."

"Sasha couldn't believe that even after hearing everything she had to say about her life, Antonio still wanted to be with her."

Sasha couldn't help but be flattered by Antonio's offer to marry her because it was clear that he cared deeply for her yet, she didn't want to tie him down or have him marry her and later regret it.

After all they had only known one another for a short time. But she figured she could still keep the baby and remain in San Antonio. This way she could continue to see Antonio and it would also provide her with the time to see whether or not he would change his mind about her and the baby.

CHAPTER FIFTEEN

Three months passed and Sasha and Antonio relationship is continuing to flourish yet, Sasha is having a lot of anxiety wondering who the father of her unborn child is.

She is also troubled by the fact that most of her life had been based upon one lie after another and she didn't want to lie to her child.

Even though Antonio had proven himself to be a mature and caring man, she still felt a need to let Justin and Tony know about her pregnancy because either of them could possibly be the father but she also knew that there were several scenarios that could backfire on her if she were to tell either

Tony or Justin about her pregnancy.

They both could exclaim that they aren't the father; they both could be happy about the news and want to be in the child's life, they could view Sasha's pregnancy as an opportunity to get back with her or they could have already moved on with their life and want nothing to do with Sasha or her baby.

Sasha believed that the best outcome for the baby was to have the father remain in her baby's life but with or without the father's involvement, she was committed to providing her baby with a healthy and loving environment.

She cared deeply for Antonio but she wasn't ready to marry him or anyone else because it was too soon after her divorce from Justin.

Although she was happy and excited about her pregnancy, Sasha was also feeling a little stupid for allowing herself to become pregnant.

After all of her years as a Call Girl, she knew perfectly well what she needed to do to avoid getting pregnant, yet she had gotten pregnant by

Justin or Tony and she felt so stupid and that she had failed all the girls at her school.

She wondered how she could counsel girls about their life when her own life is full of imperfections"

But on the other hand, Sasha thought who better to do it than someone who knows better and yet still has faults.

Sasha enjoyed working with the girls at the school and she was good at her job. Every girl that graduated from her program were either back in school or headed off to college so she had a good batting average in helping to turn girls' lives around.

But Sasha worried about what the girls would think of her, if they were to find out about her pregnancy.

Would they still view her as a role model or would they see her as a foolish older woman who with all her life experiences couldn't keep it together?

However, for Sasha, having a baby and getting pregnant at her age was not a bad thing. After all, she is in her late 30s' and the time is right for her because she is financially in good shape to provide a good life for her child.

More importantly, she is already in love with the baby she is carrying so she viewed her pregnancy as nothing short of a miracle and blessing.

Sasha believes that God has a way of stepping into our lives at just the right time to save us from ourselves or he provides us with little miracles that require nothing more than a loving home and environment.

Sasha could provide this and more so she didn't know why was she so intent on letting Justin and Tony know about her pregnancy.

She believed it was to ensure her child's father knew about the baby's existence before it is born but there was much more to her desire to be forthcoming and determined to find out about the true identity of her baby's father.

For the time being however, Sasha decided to wait until after the baby is born to seek the true identity of her child's father.

CHAPTER SIXTEEN

Six months later, Sasha gives birth to a baby girl who she names Jasmine. Throughout all of this Antonio has been right by Sasha's side and he was even in the delivery room for the birth of Sasha's baby.

He has provided her the love, comfort and understanding she needed to have a successful pregnancy and he has been less concerned about the true identity of the father of Sasha's baby and more concerned about her welfare. Antonio had assumed the role of the father in every way.

Nevertheless, for health and medical reasons relative to problems the baby could have in the future, Sasha feels that she needs to know the identity of the baby's father.

Therefore, three months later, Sasha phoned both Justin and Tony to give them the news about her baby Jasmine and she asked them if they would be willing to take a paternity test because she believes one of them is the father of her baby.

They both agreed to do the testing because they also wanted to know the answer.

It turns out that neither one of them were the father and Sasha was baffled with this finding and she thought if Justin nor Tony weren't the fathers' then who is the father of Baby Jasmine?

Then Sasha remembered the night Steve brought Justin and the other man whose name she could no longer remember for a threesome.

She was horrified by the thought of it being someone she had no real relationship with but she knew she had to find out the truth and it was more important now than ever.

Steve had been in touch with her often but Sasha was not interested in Steve as a lover so he had stopped calling her.

However, now she needed to approach Steve and requests that he take a paternity test. He too, agreed to take the test and the results were 99.99% that Steve is the father of Baby Jasmine.

Sasha didn't know how to feel about this news because there had been no real relationship with Steve except for the sexual encounters she had with him at the Manteca Inn.

She worried if Steve would try to impose himself more in her life and now she was sorry that she even bothered to have the test performed.

In the end, she knows that it was important to find out the truth and Steve has promised that he will not give Sasha any problems.

But he told Sasha that he would be there to give any love and support he could give to the baby.

However, Sasha wanted Steve to relinquish any rights to the baby because she wants to marry Antonio and have Antonio adopt the baby and carry his name.

Steve agreed with the exception that he wanted Sasha to periodically let him know about how the baby is doing.

Sasha reluctantly agrees to this request and then tells Antonio that she is now free to marry him.

However, when she gives Antonio the news, he is lukewarm about it and says he thinks they need to cool it for a while.

Sasha said, "after all we have been through and I have done to make things right to marry you and you are now saying let's cool it!"

"What's going on?"

Antonio hung his head and said, I've received some bad news today and I wasn't going to tell you about it tonight because I need time to have it sink in but I have been diagnosed with terminal cancer and I only have a few months to live. Sasha broke down crying uncontrollably. Then she jumped up from her chair and began hugging and kissing Antonio because of all the men she has loved in her life, Antonio has been the most deserving of her love and she was devastated by this horrible news.

She wanted to know if he was going to get a second opinion but the doctors were adamant that there is nothing anyone can do for him.

He had been having terrible headaches for a long time but he did nothing about it until now because he wanted to make sure that he could be in the best health for Sasha. He thought he would be given a few pills and everything would be okay.

Nevertheless, Sasha believed it more important than ever to move forward with the wedding as they had discussed.

Antonio agreed to it but told Sasha that he didn't want to be a burden to her because he knew that she had to take care of Baby Jasmine.

Even with his diagnosis, Antonio was still sensitive enough to worry and care about someone other than himself.

Antonio looked like he was fine so Sasha told him that they would deal with his sickness as it progresses and for now she just wanted to concentrate on the good in their life.

Sasha was very busy with her baby but she desperately wanted to marry Antonio before it was too late.

She asked Kelly Lismont, a sitter in her complex to care for Baby Jasmine while she made her wedding preparation.

Sasha went shopping for her wedding dress and found a beautiful white dress that hugs her voluptuous body. This is the gift she received from giving birth to Baby Jasmine.

Antonio often told her how much he loved the way she looked when she was pregnant and hoped that some of the weight that she had gained would remain after she had given birth.

Sasha hurried home with her dress excited to show it to Antonio who had agreed to come over for a special *We're Getting Married Dinner* with Sasha.

Since Kelly had agreed to keep Sasha's baby all night, she and Antonio would have the whole night to themselves without interruptions.

When Antonio showed up for dinner, he brought apple pie and ice cream.

It was the way they had begun their relationship so long ago. He grabbed Sasha and kissed her passionately.

The effects of his disease had not yet robbed him of his good looks and Antonio looked vibrant and handsome to Sasha.

But unlike before, Antonio lacked the stamina that he is so noted for but that was unimportant to her.

She loved Antonio with or without the lovemaking that they so enjoyed with one another but he was much more to her than a lovemaking machine.

He is the most decent man that Sasha has ever known. Sasha put on music and they danced the night away forgetting about the steak and potatoes that she had gone to the trouble to prepare as a special celebration dinner.

The dinner was meant to be a celebration of their love for one another. For now they simply wanted to savor every moment and not think about the little time they had left together.

The next morning, Sasha got up early to prepare breakfast while Antonio slept soundly. She returned to the bedroom with fresh fruits, eggs, sausage and toast and then called Antonio name. He was in a deep sleep, she touched him lightly to awaken him but there was no response.

Antonio was gone! Gone just like that with no goodbyes. Maybe that's why he had brought the ice cream and apple pie, Sasha wondered as she sobbed uncontrollably.

She didn't know what to do so she called 911 and they arranged for a policeman and coroner to come to Sasha's home.

When the coroner arrived to pick up Antonio's body, Sasha was hanging on to his covered body not wanting to let go of the best man she had ever had in her life.

She didn't know what she would do or how she would move on. She tried to pull herself together enough to bring Baby Jasmine home but Kelly persuaded Sasha to let Baby Jasmine remain with her for a few more days.

When Sasha hung up the telephone, she noticed Antonio sports coat dangling from the back of her sofa chair. She pulled the coat from the chair and began holding onto it, caressing and sniffing it and trying desperately to get a sniff of Antonio's good body scent.

She would always tell him how fresh and clean he smelled and the coat had his scent on it.

She knew she would never clean it because she wanted to have a part of him for as long as possible.

As she squeezed the coat more, she felt something bulging in the inside pocket of the coat. It was a notarized letter that Antonio had prepared indicating that in the advent of his death, he wanted Sasha to assume responsibility and ownership of his business.

He also had a $150,000 life insurance policy which would cover any outstanding bills he had and the remainder would go to Sasha and left $50,000 to his son from a prior relationship.

Sasha was numbed with sorrow and her heart ached so much it felt as though a hole had been made in the center of it.

She would much rather have Antonio alive than any business or money. She already had all the money she needed and right now she was thinking about how fulfilled her life was with Antonio, a simple man with an apple pie and ice cream.

Yet, in many ways, Antonio was much more. He was the sunset in her evenings, when they got together to just talk and catch up on the happenings of the day.

But mostly, he was her lover who never turned her down for lovemaking even when he had a hard day on the job.

He was willing to meet Sasha's every need and now he was gone and Sasha didn't know what she would do without him.

Sasha phoned the only other person she knew who would understand what she was going through and that was Tula.

Tula has a nurturing way about her and Sasha really needed this now. She phoned Tula and told her about everything that had happened between her and Antonio and about his death.

She also told Tula about the birth of Baby Jasmine and the unexpected father. Tula didn't ask questions, she just simply listened and provided the support Sasha needed right now.

Tula offered to come to Texas to be with Sasha and although Sasha knew that Tula was getting up in age and shouldn't be travelling, she accepted Tula's offer.

Tula wasn't worried about leaving her business for a while because she had a strong management team in place that was ready, willing and very capable of running the business until Tula returns.

Besides, there was no way Tula wouldn't be there for Sasha because Sasha was greatly responsible for the success of the Manteca Inn.

In fact, she put the Manteca on the map and she was the real reason why Tula attracted so many high caliber clients.

Sasha was known all over the world not merely for her great beauty and her intimate escapades but she was classy and took time to understand each of her clients and they greatly appreciated that about her.

It was not all about the bedroom. She was compassionate and she made all of her clients feel special.

CHAPTER SEVENTEEN

Antonio's funeral arrangements were made by his parents and Sasha understood because after all, she and Antonio hadn't been officially married and she didn't want to cause a problem with his parents so she was alone with her sorrow but so thankful that she had Tula in her life.

Tula had always been like a mother to Sasha in so many ways despite their business relationship.

At the funeral, none of Antonio's family acknowledged Sasha and that didn't matter because she knew that Antonio loved her deeply and that was her comfort now.

Tula stayed over a few more days to comfort Sasha and then headed back home to Montclair. Sasha needed to move on but didn't quite know what she would do but she had Baby Jasmine and she loved her more than life itself.

But Baby Jasmine needed a father. Antonio had agreed to fill that role and Sasha wanted him but now he was gone.

Sasha wondered should she contact Steve, should she tell him that wonderful Antonio had died or should she remain quiet and let things remain as they are?

These are the questions that Sasha wrestled with and she would take the next few months to decide. There was no need to rush answers would come in time.

For now she would spend time getting to know her baby and relishing the apple pie and ice cream that was left over from her special celebration night with Antonio.

CHAPTER EIGHTEEN

One Year Later

It has taken some time for Sasha to get to this point but she is now feeling like she is ready to take on new responsibilities and to give back to the world.

She has been very blessed with her little girl but she still misses her Dear Antonio, desperately.

Although his business was left to her, she decided not to keep control of it and turned it over to his parents.

They were grateful for her gesture. She also returned any money that he had left to her and suggested that they contribute it to a charity that had a large focus in helping to cure cancer or at least charities that work closely with cancer patients to help them lead better lives.

Steve had contacted her a while back to find out how Baby Jasmine was doing so Sasha had decided to tell him the entire truth.

He came out one weekend to offer his support but Sasha is not looking for a new relationship. She simply wants to spend as much time as she possible rebuilding her life with her baby.

However, she has not lost her desire to help others so she has made a decision to go back to the school that she operated in Montclair.

The school has done quite well without her at the helm of it but Sasha was able to bring a better perspective to the school and the girls.

She had lived the life that most of the girls were going through so she understood what made them tick and they loved her for it.

Yes, she had made a lot of mistakes but she was not going to let that keep her from giving back so she packed up everything she had and moved back home.

Everyone welcomed her with open arms. She had been through a lot much of it due to her own vulnerability and her willingness to live life without expectations.

But now she was ready to jump back into life and give it one more try.

To her surprise Tyler, Tony's daughter was now volunteering as a teen coach for troubled girls.

She immediately came up to Sasha and hugged her so tightly that Sasha thought the air would be squeezed right out of her!

She started crying and babbling about the mistake that her father had made in letting her go and Sasha told her that she didn't hold any grudges or regrets!

Tyler had heard about Sasha's new baby and she was very excited about meeting her and she was secretly holding on to hope that maybe Sasha and her father would have a chance to rekindle their relationship.

However, Sasha didn't want anything to do with Tony in that way. She has lost her best love and no one and that is no one could take his place.

For now, she was content to be back home and surrounded by people who love her.

But the next day, Tony showed up at the school to see Sasha. He had a whole lot that he wanted to apologize to her for and he wanted to do it in person because he knew that she was still angry about seeing him with another woman.

However, Sasha had long forgiven him for everything that he had done to her. It was no longer an issue because she no longer was in love with him.

But seeing Tony was very freeing for her because she was able to completely let go of her past with Tony.

She also knew that for now she didn't want to date anyone, she had been down that road and she wanted to concentrate on working with the teens to provide them with the guidance they need so that they don't end up the way she did, looking for love in the wrong people, and too caught up in the roses and champagne that she couldn't see the forest for the trees.

It wasn't until she met Antonio that she realized that expensive cars, roses and champagne mean nothing if the relationship is not built on honesty and a willingness to let your partner see your vulnerability without fear of losing the relationship.

It is then and only then that you will know that you have a true loving relationship.

ABOUT THE AUTHOR

Beverly Montgomery has always wanted to write so in her early forties, she began writing children's books and followed that up with several works of fiction, self-help booklets, poetry and a historical novel.

She has travelled extensively abroad and in the United States. She enjoys meeting people and challenging herself to do things that she has never done before.

But mostly, she enjoys writing and living vicariously through the characters she writes about.